For Imogen, Morwenna, and Finn—M.M.

For Jack and Kerenza—A.C.

First published in the United States by
Dial Books for Young Readers
A division of Penguin Young Readers Group
345 Hudson Street • New York, New York 10014
Published in Great Britain by Macmillan Children's Books
Text copyright © 2004 by Miriam Moss
Illustrations copyright © 2004 by Anna Currey
Manufactured in Belgium

5 7 9 10 8 6 4

Library of Congress Cataloging-in-Publication Data
Moss, Miriam.
Don't forget I love you / Miriam Moss ; illustrated by Anna Currey.
p.   cm.
Summary: After spending too much time playing with his favorite toy,
Billy and his mother are very late for nursery school and
his mother forgets some crucial things as she rushes to work.
ISBN 0-8037-2920-0
[1. Mother and child—Fiction. 2. Bears—Fiction.]
I. Currey, Anna, ill. II. Title.
PZ7.M85353 Do 2003   [E]—dc21
2002152119

Don't Forget I Love You

MIRIAM MOSS

Illustrated by ANNA CURREY

DIAL BOOKS FOR YOUNG READERS · NEW YORK

When Billy woke up, Rabbit was hiding
down the side of his bed.
"Don't think I can't see you there, Rabbit,"
said Billy, tugging at Rabbit's paw.

"Time for breakfast,"
Mama called from downstairs.
"In a minute," shouted Billy.
"Rabbit's being naughty."

"Come and wash
your sticky paws,"
called Mama.

"In a minute," said Billy.
"Rabbit won't eat his egg.
Hurry up, Rabbit!"

Billy and Rabbit went upstairs to get dressed.

Mama popped her head around the door.

"Get dressed, Billy," she said.

"In a minute," said Billy.

"I think Rabbit's got

a tummy ache."

"Come and brush your teeth, Billy," Mama called.

"In a minute," said Billy.
"Rabbit's buttons are all wrong."
"Get ready first, Billy,
then play with Rabbit," said Mama.

"Ready at last!" said Mama. "But where did I put your boots?"

"They're on my feet," laughed Billy.

"Oh, good." Mama smiled. "Here's your coat. Come on.
We really must go or we'll be late!"

But Billy dashed upstairs.
"Just a minute!" he called.
"Rabbit hasn't said good-bye to the others."

On the way to nursery school, Billy balanced Rabbit and his
lunch box on his head. "Be careful," said Mama.
"I am," said Billy, "except Rabbit won't sit still."

Suddenly, Billy's lunch box hit the ground and burst open.

"Oh, Billy!" said Mama crossly.
"Now we really will be late.

Give Rabbit to me and let's get a move on."

But they were very late and had to
run the rest of the way to school.

"Ah, there you are," said Mrs. Brown. "We wondered where you were."
"Sorry," panted Mama. "I have to go, I'm late for work already. Bye, Billy."
And she hurried away.

Billy hung his coat up. "Is something the matter, Billy?" asked Mrs. Brown. "Mama didn't say *I love you*," said Billy. "She always says *I love you*."

"Well, she was in a bit of a hurry,"
said Mrs. Brown.

"Have you left Rabbit by your coat?
He'll make you feel better."

They looked in Billy's pockets and even in his lunch box.

But Rabbit was nowhere to be found.

"You must have left him at home," said Mrs. Brown.

"But I didn't," said Billy, starting to cry. "I dropped my lunch box and we had to run and now Rabbit's lost and I want my mama."

At that moment the door flew open.
It was Mama!
"Oh Billy, I'm so sorry," she cried.
"I forgot to give Rabbit back to you, and
I forgot something else, too . . .

"I forgot to say *I love you*."

Billy climbed onto Mama's lap and gently she dried his tears.

"I love you, too," said Billy.
And they gave each other
a big, big hug.